Angus
and the Ducks

TOLD AND PICTURED BY
MARJORIE FLACK

A Sunburst Book · Farrar, Straus and Giroux

Once there was a very young little dog whose name was Angus, because his mother and his father came from Scotland.

Although the rest of Angus was quite small, his head was very large and so were his feet.

Angus was curious about many places and many things:

He was curious about WHAT lived under the sofa and in dark corners and

WHO was the little dog in the mirror.

He was curious about Things-Which-Come-Apart and those Things-Which-Don't-Come-Apart; such as SLIPPERS and gentlemen's SUSPENDERS

and things like that.

Angus was also curious about Things-Outdoors but he could not find out much about them because of a leash.

The leash was fastened at one end to the collar around his neck and at the other end to **SOMEBODY ELSE.**

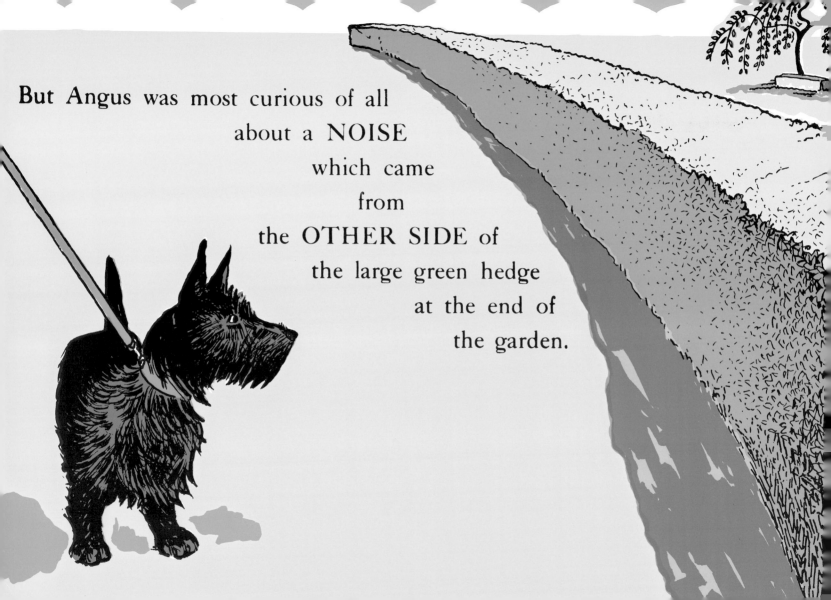

But Angus was most curious of all
about a NOISE
which came
from
the OTHER SIDE of
the large green hedge
at the end of
the garden.

The noise usually sounded like this:
Quack!   Quack!   Quackety!
        Quack!!

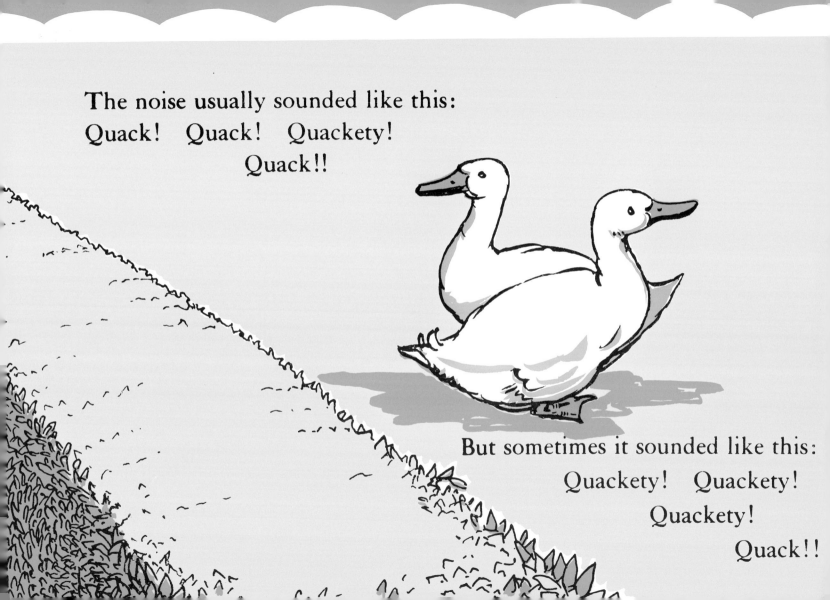

But sometimes it sounded like this:
    Quackety!   Quackety!
            Quackety!
                Quack!!

One day the door between OUTDOORS and INDOORS was left open by mistake; and out went Angus without the leash or SOMEBODY ELSE.

Down the little path he ran until he
came to the large green hedge at the end
of the garden.

He tried to go around it but it was much
too long.   He tried to go over it but it was much
too high.   So Angus went under the large green hedge
and came

out on the OTHER SIDE.

There, directly in front of

…re two white DUCKS.
…hey were marching forward,
…e-foot-up and one-foot-
down.

…ack! Quack!

Quackety!

Quack!!!

Angus said:

WOO-OO-OOF!!!

Away went the DUCKS all of a flutter.

Quackety!   Quackety!

Quackety!   Quackety!

Quackety!!!

Angus followed after.

Soon the DUCKS stopped by a stone watering trough under a mulberry tree.

Angus stopped, too. Each DUCK dipped a yellow bill in the clear cool water.   Angus watched. Each DUCK took a long drink of the cool clear water.   Still Angus watched.   Each DUCK took another long drink of cool clear water.

Then Angus said:

WOO-OO-OOF!!!

Away the DUCKS scuttled and

Angus lapped the cool clear water.

Birds sang in the mu berry tree.

The Sun made patterr through the leaves over the grass.

The DUCKS talked together:

Quack! Quack!

Quack!

Then:

HISS-S-S-S-S-S-S!!!

HISS-S-S-S-S-S-S!!!

The first DUCK nipped Angus's tail!

HISS-S-S-S-S-S-S!!!

HISS-S-S-S-S-S-S!!!

The second DUCK
flapped his
wings!

Angus scrambled under the large green hedge,

scurried up the little path,

scampered into the house

and crawled under the sofa.

For exactly THREE minutes

by the clock, Angus was

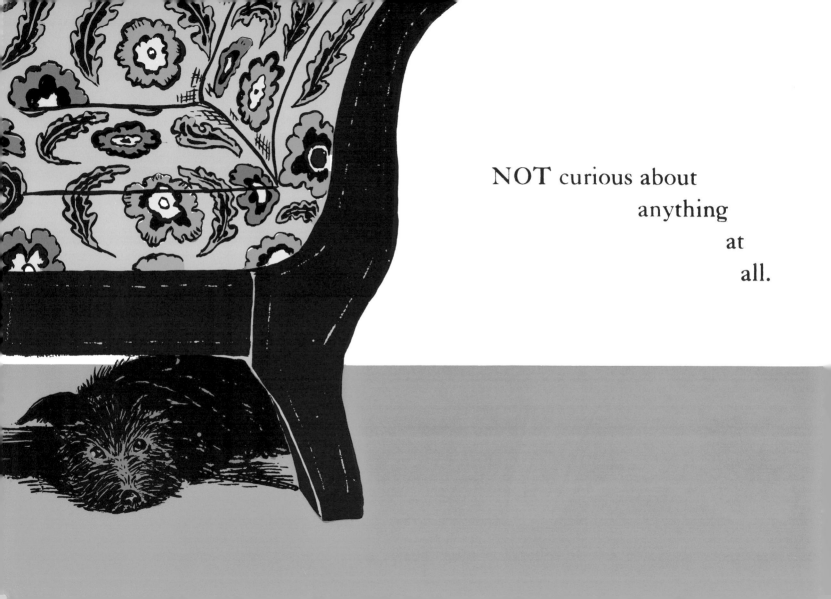

NOT curious about
anything
at
all.

E
FLACK   Flack, Marjorie
           Angus and the Ducks